CRACKING THE CODE OF HEART

A SILICON VALLEY LOVE TRIANGLE

AYUSH GEMINI

Made with ♥ on the Notion Press Platform
www.notionpress.com

For the seekers of love who navigate the labyrinth of modern romance with grace and determination, and for the visionaries who dare to dream amidst the chaos of Silicon Valley. Your courage and perseverance have inspired this tale, a tribute to the enduring strength of the human spirit and the timeless allure of love.

Contents

Contents

Foreword

Welcome to "Cracking the Code of Heart: A Silicon Valley Love Triangle."

In this captivating tale, we embark on a journey into the heart of Silicon Valley, where innovation and ambition collide with matters of the heart. Through the lens of our protagonists, we explore the complexities of love, ambition, and personal growth in a landscape defined by technological advancement and societal pressures.

As readers, we are invited to witness the intertwining lives of Ella, Alex, and Lena, each navigating their own path in the fast-paced world of technology. Their journey is one of self-discovery, as they confront their fears, chase their dreams, and ultimately come to understand the true meaning of love and sacrifice.

Set against the backdrop of Silicon Valley, this story is a reflection of the times we live in—a world where connections are made through screens, and the boundaries between virtual and reality blur. Yet, amidst the chaos of innovation and progress, the human heart remains steadfast, yearning for connection, understanding, and love.

As you delve into the pages of this book, may you find yourself captivated by the trials and triumphs of our characters, and may their journey inspire you to reflect on your own relationships and aspirations. For ultimately, "Cracking the Code of Heart" is a testament to the enduring power of love, and the belief that no matter the challenges we face, love will always find a way.

So sit back, dear reader, and prepare to embark on a journey of love, adventure, and discovery. The heart of Silicon Valley awaits, and within its depths lie the answers to life's greatest mysteries—waiting to be cracked, one code at a time.

Warm regards,
Ayush Gemini

Preface

Dear Reader,

Welcome to "Cracking the Code of Heart: A Silicon Valley Love Triangle." As you embark on this literary journey, I invite you to immerse yourself in the vibrant world of Silicon Valley, where innovation and romance intersect in unexpected ways.

The inspiration for this book came from my own experiences navigating the dynamic landscape of the tech industry. In Silicon Valley, where brilliant minds come together to push the boundaries of what's possible, I discovered a rich tapestry of stories waiting to be told—a tapestry woven with threads of ambition, passion, and, of course, love.

Through the characters of Ella, Alex, and Lena, I sought to explore the multifaceted nature of relationships in the modern era. Each character brings their own hopes, dreams, and insecurities to the table, creating a dynamic interplay of emotions that will keep you turning the pages.

But "Cracking the Code of Heart" is more than just a love story set against the backdrop of Silicon Valley—it's a reflection of the human experience in all its complexity. It's about the choices we make, the risks we take, and the profound impact that love can have on our lives.

As you delve into the pages of this book, I hope you'll find moments of laughter, tears, and everything in between. And perhaps, along the way, you'll discover something about yourself and the world around you.

Thank you for joining me on this journey. May it be as unforgettable for you as it has been for me.

Warmest regards,
Ayush Gemini

Acknowledgements

I am deeply grateful to everyone who has contributed to the creation of "Cracking the Code of Heart: A Silicon Valley Love Triangle." Writing this book has been a labor of love, and I couldn't have done it without the support and encouragement of so many wonderful people.

First and foremost, I would like to express my heartfelt thanks to my family for their unwavering support throughout this journey. Your love, encouragement, and understanding have been my rock, and I am endlessly grateful for your belief in me.

I am also indebted to my friends and colleagues who have been with me every step of the way. Your enthusiasm and feedback have been invaluable, and I am fortunate to have such an incredible support system.

A special thank you to my editor and publishing team for their guidance and expertise in bringing this book to life. Your dedication to excellence has truly made this project shine, and I am grateful for the opportunity to work with such talented professionals.

Last but not least, I would like to express my deepest gratitude to the readers who have embraced this story with open hearts. Your passion and enthusiasm for "Cracking the Code of Heart" inspire me to continue writing, and I am honored to share this journey with you.

Thank you, from the bottom of my heart, for being a part of this adventure.

Warmest regards,
Ayush Gemini

Prologue

In the heart of Silicon Valley, where innovation pulses through the streets and dreams are forged in lines of code, lies a world where love and ambition collide. It is a world of bright minds and bold ideas, where the future is shaped with each keystroke and every algorithm holds the promise of change.

Amidst the towering skyscrapers and bustling cafes, we find our protagonists—Ella, Alex, and Lena—each with their own dreams and desires, each on a journey of discovery that will test their resolve and redefine their notions of love.

For Ella, a talented but insecure software developer, Silicon Valley represents both opportunity and challenge. As she navigates the male-dominated tech industry, she grapples with self-doubt and uncertainty, yearning to prove herself in a world that often feels like a battlefield.

Alex, a seasoned programmer whose wisdom and guidance offer Ella a glimmer of hope in the midst of uncertainty. With his warm smile and reassuring presence, Alex becomes not only Ella's mentor but also the object of her affection, igniting a spark that neither can deny.

But lurking in the shadows is Lena, the ambitious project manager whose sharp tongue and competitive spirit pose a threat to Ella's dreams. As tensions rise and emotions flare, a love triangle emerges, testing the bonds of friendship and loyalty in ways none of them could have imagined.

In this melting pot of innovation and ambition, Ella's journey unfolds against the backdrop of Silicon Valley's relentless pursuit of progress. From the neon-lit streets of San Francisco to the sprawling campuses of tech giants, she navigates a world where success is measured not only by the lines of code written but also by the relationships forged along the way.

As Ella immerses herself in the fast-paced world of tech, she grapples with the complexities of workplace dynamics and the constant pressure to prove herself in a field dominated by men. Yet, beneath her quiet exterior, lies a fierce determination and a relentless drive to succeed, fueled by a burning passion for technology and a desire to make her mark on the world.

Alex, a seasoned veteran of the tech industry whose reputation precedes him. With a keen intellect and a knack for problem-solving, he quickly rose through the ranks, earning the respect and admiration of his peers. But beneath his confident facade, Alex harbored his own insecurities, haunted by the ghosts of his past and the fear of failure.

When Ella first crossed paths with Alex, she was immediately drawn to his warmth and authenticity. Despite his status as a senior programmer, Alex treated her as an equal, offering guidance and support without a hint of condescension. Their burgeoning friendship soon blossomed into something more—a connection that transcended the boundaries of mentorship and sparked a flame of longing deep within Ella's heart.

But amidst the backdrop of their budding romance, a shadow loomed on the horizon. Lena, the enigmatic project manager with a reputation for ruthlessness, cast a cold gaze upon Ella's aspirations, viewing her as nothing more than a threat to her own ambitions. With her sharp wit and piercing intellect, Lena wielded her influence like a weapon, determined to maintain her position of power at any cost.

As tensions mounted and emotions swirled, a love triangle emerged—a tangled web of desire, jealousy, and ambition that threatened to tear their world apart. Caught in the crossfire, Ella, Alex, and Lena found themselves entangled in a complex web of emotions, each struggling to reconcile their heart's desires with the harsh realities of the world around them.

In "Cracking the Code of Heart: A Silicon Valley Love Triangle," we embark on a journey of love, ambition, and self-discovery—a journey that will test the limits of their courage and resilience. And as we delve into the depths of their hearts and minds, we discover that in Silicon Valley, as in life, the greatest challenges often lead to the most profound moments of growth and transformation.

As Ella's journey unfolds amidst the fast-paced world of Silicon Valley, we witness the highs and lows of her quest for success and love. From late nights spent coding in dimly lit offices to moments of quiet reflection beneath the glow of the city lights, we accompany her on a journey of self-discovery and personal growth.

For Ella, the path to success is not without its obstacles. As she strives to prove herself in a male-dominated industry, she faces countless challenges and setbacks, each testing her resolve and pushing her to the brink of despair. Yet, through it all, she remains steadfast in her determination to succeed, fueled by a burning passion for technology and a desire to make a difference in the world.

Alex, the seasoned programmer whose presence offers Ella a beacon of hope in the midst of uncertainty. With his unwavering support and genuine kindness, he becomes not only her mentor but also her confidant, guiding her through the trials and tribulations of life in Silicon Valley.

But as their relationship deepens, tensions begin to simmer beneath the surface, threatening to unravel the delicate balance of their friendship. With Lena's shadow looming on the horizon, Ella and Alex find themselves caught in a whirlwind of emotions, each struggling to reconcile their feelings with the harsh realities of the world around them.

Meanwhile, Lena, the ambitious project manager with a reputation for ruthlessness, sets her sights on Ella, viewing her as a threat to her own ambitions. With her sharp wit and piercing intellect, Lena stops at nothing to maintain her position of power, manipulating those around her to further her own agenda.

As tensions rise and emotions flare, a love triangle emerges—a tangled web of desire, jealousy, and ambition that threatens to tear their world apart. Caught in the crossfire, Ella, Alex, and Lena find themselves entangled in a complex web of emotions, each struggling to navigate the treacherous waters of love and ambition.

In the heart of Silicon Valley, where dreams are forged in lines of code and innovation pulses through the streets, Ella, Alex, and Lena embark on a journey of love, ambition, and self-discovery—a journey that will test the limits of their courage and resilience. And as they navigate the complexities of life in the tech industry, they discover that in Silicon Valley, as in life, the greatest challenges often lead to the most profound moments of growth and transformation.

So join us, dear reader, as we venture into the heart of Silicon Valley, where love is the ultimate code waiting to be cracked. In "Cracking the Code of Heart: A Silicon Valley Love Triangle," we explore the intricate dance between love and ambition, desire and duty, as our protagonists navigate the tumultuous waters of the tech industry in search of success, happiness, and fulfillment.

As we delve into the depths of their hearts and minds, we witness the highs and lows of their journey, the triumphs and tribulations that shape their destinies. And as they confront the challenges that lie ahead, they discover that in the end, it is not the destination that matters, but the journey itself—the lessons learned, the friendships forged, and the love that transcends all boundaries.

So buckle up, dear reader, and prepare to embark on a journey unlike any other—a journey of love, ambition, and self-discovery in the heart of Silicon Valley. For in the end, it is not the lines of code we write or the algorithms we create that define us, but the love we share and the connections we forge along the way.

"Dreams Take Flight: Arrival in Silicon Valley"

CHAPTER ONE

The Code of Destiny

Small-Town Beginnings

Ella's journey to Tech Innovations didn't begin on the bustling streets of Silicon Valley, but rather in the quiet simplicity of a small town nestled among the amber waves of grain in the heartland of America. Willow Creek, with its tree-lined streets and cozy neighborhoods, was the kind of place where everyone knew each other's names and time moved at a leisurely pace.

From the moment she could toddle, Ella was drawn to the glowing screen of her family's old computer, a relic from a bygone era that her father had salvaged from a garage sale. While other toddlers were content with picture books and plush toys, Ella was captivated by the pixels dancing across the screen, her chubby fingers reaching out to touch the digital world that lay beyond.

As she grew older, Ella's fascination with technology only deepened. She would spend hours poring over computer manuals and tinkering with the family's outdated software, her curiosity driving her to unravel the mysteries of the digital realm. Her parents, recognizing her innate talent, nurtured her interests, setting up a makeshift workspace in the attic where Ella could pursue her passion to her heart's content.

But it wasn't just the allure of computers and gadgets that captured Ella's imagination. Willow Creek was a town steeped in history and tradition, its streets lined with quaint storefronts and charming cafes. Ella's fondest memories were of lazy summer days spent exploring the town with her best friend Sarah, their laughter echoing through the streets as they chased fireflies and shared secrets under the starlit sky.

It was in Willow Creek's tiny library that Ella first discovered the power of words and ideas. The dusty shelves were a treasure trove of knowledge, offering glimpses into far-off lands and distant galaxies. Ella would lose herself for hours in the pages of science fiction novels and fantasy epics, her imagination soaring as she dreamed of worlds beyond her wildest imaginings.

But amidst the idyllic charm of small-town life, Ella couldn't shake the feeling of restlessness that gnawed at her soul. While Willow Creek was a place of comfort and familiarity, it was also a place of limitations—a town where dreams were whispered but seldom pursued. As Ella approached adolescence, she began to feel increasingly out of place, like a square peg in a round hole, longing for something more.

It was during her high school years that Ella's passion for technology truly blossomed. Encouraged by a supportive teacher who recognized her talent, Ella threw herself into computer science classes with a fervor bordering on obsession. She devoured every lesson, hungrily absorbing knowledge like a sponge, her mind buzzing with ideas and possibilities.

But as Ella grew older, she began to realize that the small town she called home could only offer her so much. The local library had a limited selection of books on coding and technology, and the nearest university with a computer science program was hundreds of miles away. If Ella wanted to pursue her passion and turn it into a career, she knew she would have to leave behind the familiar comforts of home and venture into the unknown.

After years of exploration and learning in the small town of Willow Creek, Ella began to realize that her thirst for knowledge and passion for technology would lead her beyond the comfort of familiar streets. As she prepared to embark on her journey to Silicon Valley, she couldn't help but recall the words of Aristotle:

"***The roots of education are bitter, but the fruit is sweet.***"

For Ella, the bitterness of leaving behind her hometown was tempered by the sweet anticipation of the opportunities and fulfillment that awaited her in the bustling world of tech innovation

The Dream Takes Flight

With a heart full of determination and a head full of dreams, Ella set her sights on Silicon Valley—the epicenter of innovation and opportunity in the tech world. It was a journey that would take her far from everything she had ever known, testing her resilience and pushing her to her limits. But Ella was undeterred, fueled by the belief that with hard work and perseverance, anything was possible.

As Ella's departure date drew near, the small town she called home buzzed with excitement and anticipation. Friends and neighbors gathered to wish her well, their voices filled with pride and admiration for the young woman who dared to chase her dreams. But amidst the excitement, there was also a twinge of sadness—a sense of loss for the familiar sights and sounds of home that Ella would soon leave behind.

With a heavy heart and a suitcase packed with hopes and dreams, Ella bid farewell to her hometown and set out on the journey of a lifetime. The road to Silicon Valley was long and winding, dotted with countless rest stops and detours along the way. But with each passing mile, Ella grew stronger and more determined, fueled by the promise of a brighter future and the chance to make her mark on the world.

Ella's journey from the quaint streets of Willow Creek to the bustling tech hub of Silicon Valley echoed the words of Ralph Waldo Emerson:

> ***"Do not go where the path may lead, go instead where there is no path and leave a trail."***

With each step she took towards her dreams, Ella blazed a trail of determination and courage, carving out her own path in a world filled with uncertainty and possibility.

The City of Dreams

Ella's journey to Silicon Valley had been a long and arduous one, filled with moments of doubt and uncertainty. But as she stepped off the plane and onto the bustling streets of the city, all of those doubts melted away, replaced by a sense of exhilaration and anticipation.

The sights and sounds of Silicon Valley were unlike anything Ella had ever experienced. Skyscrapers towered overhead, their glass facades gleaming in the sunlight. The streets pulsed with the energy of a city that never slept, a city where dreams were born and fortunes made.

Ella's heart raced as she took in the scene before her, feeling a surge of excitement at the endless possibilities that lay ahead. This was it—the moment she had been waiting for, the culmination of years of dreams and aspirations. With a smile on her face and a spring in her step, she ventured further into the heart of the city, eager to begin her new life in this vibrant metropolis.

Amidst the towering skyscrapers and bustling streets of Silicon Valley, Ella felt a sense of exhilaration wash over her—a feeling captured perfectly by Walt Disney when he said, '

> "*All our dreams can come true, if we have the courage to pursue them.*"

With each step she took into the heart of the city, Ella embraced the boundless opportunities before her, fueled by the courage to chase her dreams and turn them into reality

A New Chapter Begins

Arriving at Tech Innovations, Ella's excitement reached a fever pitch. The sleek, glass-walled building loomed before her, a beacon of innovation and progress in the heart of Silicon Valley. Stepping through the doors, she was greeted by the hum of computers and the chatter of her colleagues, the air alive with the promise of possibility.

As Ella made her way through the maze of cubicles and conference rooms, she couldn't help but feel a sense of awe. This was where the magic happened, where ideas were born and technology was shaped. The walls were adorned with motivational posters and whiteboards filled with scribbled equations, a testament to the creativity and ingenuity that thrived within these walls.

Her first interactions with her colleagues were a blur of introductions and handshakes, each one eager to welcome her to the team. Ella was struck by the diversity of the people she met—programmers and designers, engineers and marketers, each bringing their own unique skills and perspectives to the table. It was a melting pot of talent and creativity, and Ella was thrilled to be a part of it.

Ella found herself surrounded by the promise of possibility. It brought to mind the words of Steve Jobs:

> ***"The people who are crazy enough to think they can change the world are the ones who do."***

With each handshake and introduction, Ella felt the weight of those words, knowing that she was among those who dared to dream big and change the world with their innovation and determination.

As she settled into her new surroundings, surrounded by the bright lights and high-tech gadgets of the office, Ella couldn't help but feel a sense of belonging. This was where she was meant to be, among people who shared her passion for technology and innovation. With a sense of purpose and determination burning bright within her, Ella took her first steps into the world of Tech Innovations, ready to write her own destiny in lines of code and pixels of possibility.

> ***"As we journey through life, we often find ourselves at the crossroads of familiarity and possibility. It's in these moments of transition that we discover the true essence of growth and resilience. Embracing the unknown may be daunting, but it's through stepping outside our comfort zones that we unearth our greatest strengths and unlock the doors to our wildest dreams."***

-Ayush Gemini

"Navigating New Connections"

CHAPTER TWO

ENTER ALEX

A Beacon in the Chaos

As Ella navigated her way through the maze of cubicles at Tech Innovations, her nerves were on edge. Being a junior developer in a male-dominated industry was daunting, to say the least. But amidst the sea of unfamiliar faces, there was one that stood out—a beacon of calm and confidence in the chaos. His name was Alex.

Alex was a senior developer at Tech Innovations, with a reputation for brilliance tempered by a down-to-earth demeanor that made him approachable to even the most junior of employees. Tall and lean with a shock of unruly hair and a perpetual twinkle in his eye, Alex had a way of putting people at ease with his easy smile and quick wit.

Comedic Encounters

Their first meeting was a comedy of errors, a classic case of "wrong place, wrong time." Ella had been nervously fumbling with her phone in the break room, trying to navigate the company's labyrinthine intranet, when Alex appeared beside her, a steaming cup of coffee in hand and a mischievous grin on his face.

"Need a hand?" he asked, his voice laced with amusement as he peered over Ella's shoulder at her phone.

Ella blushed furiously, her cheeks flaming with embarrassment. "Oh, uh, no, I'm fine, thanks," she stammered, hastily tucking her phone away.

But Alex only laughed, his laughter infectious as he leaned against the counter, his eyes sparkling with mirth. "Come on, don't be shy," he said, nudging her gently with his elbow. "We've all been there. Trust me, the company's intranet is like a labyrinth. It takes a seasoned pro to navigate it."

Despite herself, Ella couldn't help but smile at Alex's easy charm. He had a way of making even the most awkward situations seem laughable, a talent she found both disarming and endearing.

As they worked together over the coming days and weeks, Ella found herself drawn to Alex in ways she couldn't quite explain. Their interactions were filled with playful banter and inside jokes, each one a testament to the growing chemistry between them.

> ***"Sometimes, the most profound connections begin with a simple spark—a shared glance, a fleeting smile. In those moments, we find ourselves drawn to another soul, inexplicably tethered by an invisible thread of destiny."***

- Ayush Gemini

Messages and Moments

The fluorescent lights buzzed softly overhead as Ella sat at her desk, tapping away at her keyboard with a furrowed brow. It had been a challenging morning, filled with endless lines of code and frustrating bugs that seemed determined to elude her grasp. But amidst the chaos of her workday, there was one bright spot—a message from Alex.

A notification popped up on Ella's computer screen, accompanied by a cheerful ping. She couldn't help but smile as she read the words that appeared before her:

Alex: Hey there, how's it going?

Ella: Hey! Honestly, I'm drowning in code right now. How about you?

Alex: Same here! I swear, if I have to debug one more line of code, I might lose my mind.

Ella: Haha, tell me about it. It feels like every time I fix one bug, three more pop up in its place.

Alex: Welcome to the glamorous world of software development! But hey, at least we're in it together, right?

Ella: Definitely! I don't know what I'd do without your help and guidance. You're a lifesaver, Alex.

Alex: Aw, shucks. You're making me blush over here! But seriously, if you ever need anything, just let me know. I've got your back.

As Ella read Alex's words, a warm feeling washed over her. Despite the challenges of their work, knowing that she had someone like Alex by her side made all the difference. He was more than just a mentor—he was a friend, a confidant, and maybe, just maybe, something more.

With a renewed sense of determination, Ella turned her attention back to her work, the knowledge that Alex was there to support her giving her the strength to tackle even the most daunting of tasks. And as she dove back into the sea of code before her, she couldn't help but feel a sense of excitement for the journey that lay ahead.

Unspoken Feelings

But amidst the laughter and camaraderie, there was something more—a spark of connection that went beyond mere friendship or professional courtesy. It was subtle at first, a fleeting glance or a shared smile, but as they spent more time together, it grew stronger, igniting a flame of attraction that burned bright in the darkness.

Ella tried to ignore the butterflies that fluttered in her stomach whenever she was near Alex, telling herself it was nothing more than a harmless crush. But deep down, she knew there was something more—a connection that went beyond words or logic.

As they navigated the ups and downs of office life together, Ella found herself opening up to Alex in ways she never thought possible, sharing her hopes and dreams, her fears and insecurities. And in return, Alex offered her unwavering support and encouragement, guiding her through the complexities of their shared profession with patience and grace.

But as their bond deepened, so too did the stakes. For Ella, Alex wasn't just a mentor or a friend—he was something more, something she couldn't quite put into words. And as they stood on the precipice of something new and unknown, Ella couldn't help but wonder what the future held in store for them both.

With each passing day, the chemistry between them grew stronger, until it was almost impossible to deny. And as they laughed and joked their way through the trials and tribulations of office life, Ella and Alex found themselves embarking on a journey that would change their lives forever.

"The Clash Unveiled"

CHAPTER THREE

Rivalry Revealed

The Arrival of Lena

The morning sun filtered through the windows of Tech Innovations, casting a warm glow over the bustling office. Ella stepped through the glass doors, her mind buzzing with excitement for the day ahead. Little did she know, her world was about to be turned upside down.

As she approached her cubicle, Ella noticed a figure standing beside it, her posture radiating confidence and authority. Curious, Ella quickened her pace, her curiosity piqued by the unfamiliar presence.

"Can I help you?" Ella asked, her voice tentative yet polite.

The woman turned to face her, her expression cool and composed. "You must be Ella," she stated, her voice carrying a hint of challenge. "I'm Lena, the new project manager."

Ella's heart sank at Lena's introduction. She had heard whispers about the new project manager—a formidable figure rumored to be as ambitious as she was ruthless. But nothing could have prepared her for the reality of facing Lena head-on.

Lena was no stranger to the world of technology. With a prestigious education from a top-tier university and years of experience at some of the biggest tech firms in Silicon Valley, Lena had earned a reputation as a force to be reckoned with. She was known for her sharp intellect, her unwavering determination, and her relentless pursuit of success. And now, she had set her sights on Tech Innovations.

Clash of Titans

As the days passed, tensions between Ella and Lena continued to simmer beneath the surface. What had started as a simple clash of personalities soon escalated into a full-blown rivalry, fueled by ambition and pride.

Their interactions became increasingly fraught with tension, each conversation a battle of wills between two strong-willed women. Where Ella sought collaboration and cooperation, Lena saw only competition and conflict.

One particularly tense moment occurred during a team meeting, when Ella presented her ideas for a new project. As she spoke, Lena listened with a critical eye, her gaze unwavering as she dissected Ella's proposals with ruthless precision.

"I'm not sure that's the best approach," Lena remarked, her tone dismissive. "Perhaps we should consider a more innovative strategy."

Ella felt a surge of frustration and anger at Lena's comments. She had poured her heart and soul into her ideas, only to have them torn apart by someone who seemed determined to undermine her at every turn.

But Ella refused to back down. She had worked too hard, fought too long, to let someone like Lena tear her down. And so, armed with nothing more than her determination and grit, Ella faced Lena head-on, ready to prove once and for all that she was not to be underestimated.

The atmosphere in the office was charged with tension as Lena and Ella found themselves locked in yet another heated debate. The morning sun streamed through the windows, casting long shadows across the room as their voices echoed off the walls.

"You have no idea what you're talking about," Lena's voice cut through the air like a knife, her eyes flashing with anger. "You're just a junior developer—a nobody."

Ella bristled at Lena's words, her fists clenched at her sides. She refused to let Lena's insults get to her, but the sting of her words lingered like a fresh wound.

"I may be a junior developer, but at least I'm not willing to sacrifice my integrity for the sake of winning," Ella shot back, her voice dripping with contempt.

The tension in the room was palpable as they stared each other down, neither willing to back down in the face of the other's stubbornness.

> ***"The ultimate measure of a man is not where he stands in moments of comfort and convenience, but where he stands at times of challenge and controversy."***
>
> **- Martin Luther King Jr.**

The Office Divided

Their clash of wills had become a common occurrence in the office, each confrontation more intense than the last. Where Ella saw opportunity and collaboration, Lena saw only competition and conflict. Their differing perspectives fueled the flames of their rivalry, turning every interaction into a battle for dominance.

As the weeks turned into months, the rivalry between Ella and Lena reached a fever pitch. Their clashes grew more frequent, their words more cutting, until it seemed as though the entire office was caught in the crossfire of their battle for supremacy.

Seeking Common Ground

But amidst the chaos and conflict, there was a glimmer of hope—a chance for reconciliation and understanding. For deep down, Ella knew that Lena was not her enemy, but rather a fellow warrior in the fight for success. And if they could only set aside their differences and work together, they might just find a way to conquer the challenges that lay ahead.

But that was a bridge they would have to cross another day. For now, the tension between Ella and Lena hung heavy in the air, a silent reminder of the battles yet to come.

> ***"Strength is not measured by the challenges we avoid, but by those we confront head-on, unyielding in our determination to overcome."***

- Ayush Gemini

"Amidst the Code and Conflicts: Navigating Love and Rivalry"

CHAPTER FOUR

Love in the Code

Ella and Alex's Connection

The soft glow of the computer screens illuminated the dimly lit office as Ella sat at her desk, immersed in lines of code. It was late, the rest of the office deserted as most of her colleagues had long since gone home. But for Ella, there was nowhere else she'd rather be.

As she worked, a familiar presence approached her cubicle, the gentle sound of footsteps echoing through the quiet workspace. Ella looked up to see Alex standing there, a warm smile gracing his features.

"Hey," he said softly, his voice a welcome interruption in the silence. "Burnin' the midnight oil again, huh?"

Ella chuckled, a hint of sheepishness coloring her cheeks. "Guilty as charged," she admitted. "I just can't seem to tear myself away from this project."

Alex nodded understandingly, his eyes twinkling with amusement. "I know the feeling," he said, taking a seat beside her. "There's something about coding that's just... addictive, you know?"

Ella couldn't help but smile at his words. It was true—there was a certain magic in the art of coding, a thrill that came with solving complex problems and bringing ideas to life. And in that moment, she felt a kinship with Alex unlike anything she had ever experienced before.

"The only way to do great work is to love what you do."

- Steve Jobs

As they worked side by side, their conversation flowed effortlessly, each word building a bridge between them. They spoke of their shared love for technology, swapping stories of their favorite programming languages and the projects that had inspired them.

But amidst the talk of code and algorithms, there was something deeper brewing between them—a connection that went beyond shared interests and mutual respect. It was a spark, a flicker of something more, waiting to ignite into flames.

And as the night wore on and the lines of code blurred together, Ella couldn't help but feel drawn to Alex in a way she had never felt before. There was an easiness to their conversation, a comfort that came with being in each other's presence.

It was as though they were two pieces of a puzzle, finally coming together to form a complete picture. And in that moment, Ella knew that she had found someone special—a kindred spirit who shared her passion for coding and technology, and who understood her in a way no one else ever had.

As the night stretched on and the rest of the world faded away, Ella and Alex continued to work side by side, their connection growing stronger with each passing moment. And as the first light of dawn broke through the darkness, they knew that this was only the beginning of their journey together.

Navigating Workplace Romance

As the days passed, Ella found herself increasingly drawn to Alex, her thoughts filled with memories of their late-night coding sessions and heartfelt conversations. But amidst the growing attraction, Ella couldn't shake the nagging feeling of uncertainty that lingered in the back of her mind.

The complexities of workplace romance weighed heavily on Ella's shoulders as she struggled to navigate her feelings for Alex while maintaining professionalism in the office. She knew that crossing the line between colleagues and something more could jeopardize not only her career but also the dynamic of their team.

Caught in a whirlwind of emotions, Ella found herself torn between her heart and her head. On one hand, there was the undeniable chemistry between her and Alex—the shared glances, the lingering touches, the unspoken words that hung between them like a veil of anticipation. But on the other hand, there were the whispered warnings of caution, the fear of risking it all for the sake of fleeting romance.

As Ella grappled with her internal conflict, she found herself seeking solace in the familiarity of her work. Coding became her refuge, a sanctuary where she could lose herself in lines of code and algorithms, away from the complexities of her heart.

But try as she might, Ella couldn't escape the growing tension between her and Alex. Their interactions became charged with an undercurrent of longing, each moment tinged with the unspoken desire that simmered beneath the surface.

And as the days turned into weeks, Ella knew that she could no longer ignore the truth of her feelings. She was falling for Alex, hard and fast, and there was nothing she could do to stop it.

But with great risk came great reward, and Ella found herself torn between the allure of love and the fear of what lay ahead. Would she dare to take the leap, to follow her heart and see where it led? Or would she retreat into the safety of familiarity, choosing to protect her heart rather than risk it all for the chance at something more?

As she pondered her options, Ella couldn't help but wonder what the future held in store. Whatever path she chose, one thing was certain—the complexities of workplace romance had become all too apparent, and Ella knew that she would have to tread carefully if she wanted to navigate the rocky terrain of love in the code.

"***In the end, we only regret the chances we didn't take.***"

- Lewis Carroll

Lena's Animosity

While Ella wrestled with her feelings for Alex, another player entered the fray, casting a shadow over their budding romance. Lena, the ambitious project manager, harbored a secret crush on Alex—a crush that fueled her animosity towards Ella and added another layer of tension to their dynamic.

From the moment Lena had laid eyes on Alex, she had been captivated by his charm and intelligence. His easy smile and unwavering confidence had drawn her in, igniting a spark of desire that she couldn't ignore.

But as Lena's feelings for Alex grew, so too did her resentment towards Ella. In her eyes, Ella was nothing more than an obstacle—a rival for Alex's attention, standing in the way of what Lena wanted most.

Their interactions became increasingly strained, each conversation laced with thinly veiled hostility.But despite Ella's best efforts to rise above Lena's animosity, the tension between them continued to simmer beneath the surface, threatening to boil over at any moment.

As Ella's connection with Alex deepened, a subtle shift occurred in the office dynamics—a shift fueled by Lena's growing resentment towards Ella.

It was during a team brainstorming session that tensions finally reached a boiling point. Ella had just finished outlining her proposal for a new project when Lena interrupted with a dismissive scoff.

"I'm sorry, but that idea just won't cut it," Lena declared, her tone dripping with contempt. "We need something more innovative, something that will truly push the boundaries of what's possible."

Ella felt a flush of anger rise in her cheeks at Lena's dismissive tone, but she held her tongue, determined not to let Lena's hostility get the best of her.

But Lena wasn't finished. With a pointed glance in Ella's direction, she continued, "Maybe if you spent less time trying to impress Alex and more time focusing on your work, you'd actually come up with something worthwhile."

The words hit Ella like a slap in the face, her heart sinking at Lena's thinly veiled attack. She knew that Lena's resentment towards her had been simmering beneath the surface for some time, but she had never expected it to manifest in such a public and humiliating manner.

As the tension in the room thickened, Ella felt a surge of defiance rise within her. She squared her shoulders and met Lena's gaze head-on, refusing to back down in the face of her adversary's hostility.

"I stand by my proposal," Ella declared, her voice steady and unwavering. "And I won't let anyone undermine my contributions to this team, least of all you."

The room fell silent at Ella's words, the weight of her defiance hanging heavy in the air. It was a moment of reckoning, a clash of wills that laid bare the simmering resentment and animosity that had been festering between them for far too long.

But amidst the tension and hostility, there was also a glimmer of something else—a flicker of determination and strength that burned bright within Ella's heart. She may have been faced with adversity, but she refused to let it break her.

And as she stood her ground in the face of Lena's hostility, Ella knew that she was stronger than she had ever been before. No matter what challenges lay ahead, she was ready to face them head-on, armed with nothing but her courage and her conviction.

And as Ella grappled with her feelings for Alex and navigated the treacherous waters of workplace politics, she couldn't help but wonder what the future held in store. Would she and Alex find a way to overcome the obstacles standing in their way, or would Lena's growing crush on Alex tear them apart before they ever had a chance to explore their feelings for each other?

As she pondered these questions, Ella knew that one thing was certain—the road to love in the code would be anything but smooth, and she would have to tread carefully if she wanted to navigate the rocky terrain ahead.

"You may encounter many defeats, but you must not be defeated."

- Maya Angelou

"Turbulence in the Workplace: Navigating Love, Hostility, and Inner Struggle"

CHAPTER FIVE

LINES BLURRED

Insecurity and Doubt

The atmosphere in the office felt charged with tension as Ella sat at her desk, her fingers hovering over the keyboard, unable to focus on the task at hand. The events of the past few days had left her feeling raw and vulnerable, her emotions swirling like a tempest within her.

It was during a routine team meeting that the incident occurred—a seemingly innocuous exchange that sent shockwaves through Ella's already fragile sense of security.

As Ella presented her ideas for an upcoming project, she couldn't help but notice the subtle glances exchanged between Alex and Lena. They were fleeting, barely noticeable to anyone else, but to Ella, they were like a knife to the heart.

She tried to brush off the unease that gnawed at her insides, to convince herself that she was simply imagining things. But the doubt lingered, festering like an open wound that refused to heal.

As the meeting drew to a close, Ella found herself lingering behind, unable to tear herself away from the suffocating atmosphere of the conference room. She watched in silence as Alex and Lena engaged in animated conversation, their laughter ringing in her ears like a cruel taunt.

And then, in a moment that would haunt her for days to come, Lena reached out to touch Alex's arm, a playful smile dancing on her lips. It was a simple gesture, easily dismissed by anyone else. But for Ella, it was the final straw.

Her heart sank like a stone in her chest as she watched the exchange unfold before her eyes. She felt a surge of anger and betrayal, followed by a crushing wave of self-doubt. Was she imagining things, or was there truly something between Alex and Lena that she couldn't see?

The questions swirled in Ella's mind, each one more relentless than the last. She felt like a puppet on strings, pulled in a hundred different directions by the conflicting emotions that raged within her.

And as she finally tore herself away from the scene unfolding before her, Ella knew that she couldn't ignore the truth any longer. The lines between friendship and romance had blurred beyond recognition, and she was caught in the crossfire, unsure of which way to turn.

"***Adversity introduces a man to himself.***"

- Albert Einstein

Escalating Hostility

As tensions continued to mount in the office, Lena's hostility towards Ella reached a crescendo, culminating in a confrontation that left Ella questioning her place in the company and her relationship with Alex.

It was a typical Wednesday afternoon when the incident occurred—a seemingly mundane day that would forever be etched in Ella's memory.

As Ella sat at her desk, engrossed in her work, she couldn't shake the feeling of being watched. Glancing up, she met Lena's steely gaze, her eyes narrowed with barely concealed contempt.

"Ella, can I speak with you for a moment?" Lena's voice cut through the silence like a knife, sending a shiver down Ella's spine.

Nervously, Ella rose from her desk and followed Lena to a secluded corner of the office, her heart pounding in her chest.

"What's this about, Lena?" Ella asked, trying to keep her voice steady despite the rising sense of unease.

But Lena's response was anything but reassuring. With a cold smile, she launched into a scathing tirade, accusing Ella of incompetence and insubordination in front of their colleagues.

"You're a liability to this team, Ella," Lena spat, her words dripping with venom. "Your work is subpar, and your attitude is unacceptable. If you can't step up and meet the standards of this company, then perhaps it's time for you to find employment elsewhere."

Ella felt like she had been punched in the gut, the weight of Lena's words crushing her spirit beneath their weight. She had always known that Lena harbored animosity towards her, but she had never expected it to manifest in such a public and humiliating manner.

As Lena's tirade continued, Ella felt the eyes of her colleagues boring into her, their silent judgment weighing heavily on her shoulders. She wanted to defend herself, to stand up to Lena and prove her wrong. But the words caught in her throat, suffocated by the overwhelming sense of shame and humiliation that threatened to consume her whole.

And then, just as suddenly as it had begun, the confrontation was over. Lena stormed off in a flurry of anger, leaving Ella standing alone in the aftermath of the storm.

As she made her way back to her desk, Ella couldn't shake the feeling of being adrift in a sea of uncertainty. Lena's words echoed in her mind, taunting her with their cruelty and disdain.

But amidst the chaos and confusion, there was one thing Ella knew for certain—she would not let Lena's hostility break her. She may have been bruised and battered, but she refused to be defeated. With a newfound determination burning bright within her, Ella vowed to rise above the turmoil and prove her worth to the company, no matter what obstacles lay in her path.

Alex's Inner Conflict

In the midst of the swirling tensions and escalating drama, Alex found himself grappling with a tumultuous inner conflict—a battle between his growing feelings for Ella and his commitment to maintaining professionalism in the workplace.

It was a conflict that had been brewing beneath the surface for weeks, simmering like a pot ready to boil over. And as the tension between Ella, Lena, and himself reached new heights, Alex found himself teetering on the edge of a precipice, unsure of which way to turn.

On one hand, there was Ella—a bright light in the darkness, a beacon of hope in the tumultuous sea of office politics. From the moment he had met her, Alex had been drawn to her infectious enthusiasm and unwavering determination. He admired her resilience in the face of adversity, her willingness to stand up for herself and what she believed in.

But as their relationship deepened, so too did Alex's fears. He knew that becoming involved with a coworker was fraught with risks, that it could jeopardize not only their careers but the dynamic of the entire team. And as much as he longed to explore his feelings for Ella, he couldn't shake the nagging voice in the back of his mind that warned him of the potential consequences.

And then there was Lena—a force of nature in her own right, with a charm and charisma that drew people to her like moths to a flame. Alex couldn't deny the attraction he felt towards her, the way her presence seemed to fill the room with electricity.

But beneath the surface, there was something darker—a ruthlessness and ambition that bordered on obsession. And as Lena's hostility towards Ella intensified, Alex found himself torn between his loyalty to his colleague and his growing disillusionment with her behavior.

It was a delicate balancing act, one that threatened to unravel at any moment. And as Alex struggled to navigate the treacherous waters of office politics and personal relationships, he couldn't help but feel the weight of the world bearing down on his shoulders.

But amidst the chaos and uncertainty, there was one thing Alex knew for certain—he couldn't ignore his feelings for Ella any longer. She had become a beacon of light in his life, a source of strength and inspiration in the darkest of times. And no matter what challenges lay ahead, he was determined to fight for their chance at happiness, even if it meant risking everything he had worked so hard to achieve.

And so, with a heavy heart and a steely resolve, Alex braced himself for the storm that was sure to come, knowing that the road ahead would be anything but easy. But as long as he had Ella by his side, he knew that together, they could weather any storm that came their way.

"In the crucible of adversity, our resolve is tested, and our character forged. As we navigate the turbulent waters of uncertainty and doubt, we must remember that it is our inner strength and resilience that will guide us through the storm. For it is not the challenges we face that define

***us, but how we rise to meet them.*"**

- Ayush Gemini

"Fury and Resolve: The Clash of Titans and the Fragile Balance of Love"

CHAPTER SIX

Conflict on the Horizon

Clash of Titans

The air in the office crackled with tension as Ella and Lena found themselves on a collision course, their clash over a high-stakes project threatening to ignite a firestorm that would consume them both.

It had been building for weeks—a simmering feud fueled by jealousy, resentment, and a fierce determination to come out on top. And now, as they stood face to face, the tension between them was palpable, like a storm gathering on the horizon, ready to unleash its fury.

The project in question was a make-or-break endeavor for the company, a chance to showcase their innovation and expertise on a global stage. And with the eyes of their colleagues and superiors watching their every move, the pressure to succeed was more intense than ever before.

But for Ella and Lena, the project represented something more—a battleground where they could settle their scores once and for all, where they could prove once and for all who was truly worthy of Alex's attention and admiration.

As they squared off in the conference room, the atmosphere crackled with electricity, each word a dagger aimed at the other's heart. Lena's voice dripped with scorn as she tore apart Ella's ideas, dismissing them as amateurish and uninspired.

"You really think this is the best you can do, Ella?" Lena taunted, her eyes glittering with malice. "I expected more from someone who claims to be a rising star in this company. But I suppose talent can only take you so far when you lack the vision and creativity to back it up."

Ella felt a surge of anger and frustration rise within her at Lena's cutting words. She knew that Lena's criticisms were unfounded, that her ideas were solid and well-researched. But try as she might, she couldn't shake the feeling of doubt that gnawed at her insides, threatening to undermine her confidence and resolve.

And then, in a moment of pure recklessness, Ella lashed out, her words sharp and biting as she defended her ideas with a fervor born of desperation.

"You may have the title of project manager, Lena, but that doesn't give you the right to belittle and undermine your colleagues," Ella retorted, her voice trembling with pent-up emotion. "If you want to criticize my work, then do it constructively. But don't expect me to sit back and take your insults lying down."

The room fell silent at Ella's outburst, the tension thickening like a heavy fog. It was a moment of reckoning, a clash of wills that laid bare the simmering resentment and animosity that had been festering between them for far too long.

And as Ella and Lena stood locked in a battle of wills, the fate of the project—and their professional reputations—hung in the balance. It was a moment that would define their careers, a test of strength and resilience that would push them to their limits and beyond.

A Heart Divided

The office hummed with the energy of impending conflict as Ella and Lena's rivalry escalated to new heights. Alex, caught in the middle, found himself torn between his loyalty to his colleague and the growing realization of his feelings for Ella.

One incident, in particular, stood out in Alex's mind—a tense meeting that had quickly devolved into a heated argument between Ella and Lena. As the two women sparred over the direction of the project, Alex struggled to maintain his composure, his heart torn between the two sides.

"Ella, I really think we should consider taking a different approach," Lena suggested, her tone laced with thinly veiled condescension.

But Ella wasn't about to back down. "I respectfully disagree, Lena. I believe my proposal offers the best solution for our needs."

The tension in the room was palpable as the argument raged on, each side digging in their heels and refusing to concede an inch. Alex felt like a spectator at a tennis match, his head spinning as he tried to keep up with the volley of words and accusations flying back and forth.

But amidst the chaos, there was one moment that stood out—a fleeting glance between Ella and Alex that spoke volumes without a single word being uttered. In that brief exchange, Alex saw the raw emotion reflected in Ella's eyes—the fear, the determination, the unwavering resolve to stand her ground no matter the cost.

And in that moment, something inside Alex shifted. He realized that he couldn't stand idly by and watch as Ella fought alone against the tide of adversity. He had to make a choice—a choice to stand by her side and fight for what they believed in, no matter the consequences.

With a newfound sense of purpose and determination, Alex squared his shoulders and prepared to face the storm head-on. Whatever lay ahead, he knew that as long as he had Ella by his side, they could weather any challenge that came their way.

The Tipping Point

As tensions between Ella and Lena continued to escalate, the delicate balance of their relationships hung precariously in the air, threatening to unravel at any moment. With each passing day, the atmosphere in the office grew more charged, the animosity between the two women reaching a fever pitch.

It all came to a head one fateful afternoon, during a crucial meeting to discuss the progress of the project. As Ella presented her latest ideas to the team, Lena's hostility boiled over, her thinly veiled contempt spilling out like venom.

"I'm sorry, Ella, but I just don't see how your proposal is feasible," Lena interjected, her voice dripping with disdain. "It's clear that you're out of your depth here. Maybe it's time for you to step aside and let someone with more experience take the reins."

Ella bristled at Lena's words, her hands clenched into fists at her sides. But before she could respond, Alex stepped in, his voice calm but firm as he addressed the room.

"That's enough, Lena," Alex said, his tone leaving no room for argument. "Ella's ideas are just as valid as anyone else's here. We're a team, and we need to work together if we want to succeed."

But Lena wasn't about to back down. With a sneer, she turned to face Alex, her eyes flashing with anger. "And what would you know about success, Alex? You've been too busy playing mentor to Ella to focus on the real work at hand. Maybe it's time for you to choose where your loyalties truly lie."

The room fell silent at Lena's words, the tension thickening like a heavy fog. It was a moment of reckoning, a dramatic confrontation that would change everything.

Caught in the middle of the chaos, Alex felt the weight of the world bearing down on his shoulders. He knew that whatever decision he made in that moment would have far-reaching consequences, not just for himself, but for everyone involved.

But amidst the chaos and uncertainty, there was one thing Alex knew for certain—he couldn't stand by and watch as Ella's dreams were crushed beneath the weight of Lena's ambition. With a steely resolve and a determination to protect the woman he loved, Alex braced himself for the storm that was sure to come, knowing that whatever lay ahead, they would face it together.

As the confrontation reached its peak, emotions ran high and tempers flared. Ella, her patience worn thin by Lena's constant undermining, finally spoke out, her voice trembling with a mixture of anger and frustration.

"I won't let you tear us apart, Lena," Ella declared, her eyes blazing with defiance. "We're a team, and we're stronger together. No amount of petty jealousy or manipulation will change that."

Lena's mask of confidence slipped for a moment, her facade crumbling in the face of Ella's unwavering resolve. But before she could respond, the sound of a phone ringing shattered the tense silence, bringing the meeting to an abrupt halt.

It was a moment of reprieve—a brief respite from the chaos and conflict that had engulfed them all. But as the ringing continued, echoing like a harbinger of doom in the stillness of the room, Alex knew that their troubles were far from over.

With a heavy heart and a sense of foreboding weighing on his mind, Alex braced himself for the storm that was sure to come, knowing that the decisions made in the coming days would shape the course of their futures in ways they could scarcely imagine.

And as the meeting adjourned and the team dispersed, Alex found himself alone with his thoughts, grappling with the weight of the choices that lay before him. Should he stand by Ella's side and risk everything for love, or should he heed Lena's warning and distance himself from the conflict, preserving his career at the expense of his heart?

It was a question that gnawed at him, twisting like a knife in his gut as he wrestled with his inner demons. But amidst the turmoil and uncertainty, one thing remained clear—no matter what path he chose, the consequences would be profound, and the repercussions far-reaching.

With a heavy heart and a mind swirling with doubt, Alex braced himself for the storm that was sure to come, knowing that the decisions made in the coming days would shape the course of their futures in ways they could scarcely imagine.

And as he stepped out into the cold night air, the weight of the world pressing down on his shoulders, Alex knew that he was facing the most difficult decision of his life—a decision that would test not only his loyalty and integrity but his very sense of self.

The Fragile Balance

As tensions between Ella, Alex, and Lena continued to mount, the fragile balance of their relationships teetered on the edge of collapse. Every interaction was fraught with tension, every word laden with unspoken meaning. It was as if the very air in the office crackled with the intensity of their simmering conflict.

Ella felt the weight of Lena's hostility bearing down on her like a suffocating blanket, her every move scrutinized and criticized. It seemed that no matter what she did, she couldn't escape Lena's relentless scrutiny, her constant attempts to undermine her confidence and belittle her achievements.

And yet, despite Lena's best efforts, Ella refused to back down. She knew that she had just as much right to be there as anyone else, that her skills and talents were just as valuable as those of her colleagues. And she was determined to prove it, no matter the cost.

But as the tension between Ella and Lena reached its breaking point, Alex found himself caught in the middle, torn between his loyalty to his friend and his growing feelings for Ella. It was a position he never wanted to be in, a conflict of interest that threatened to tear him apart.

And then, one fateful day, it all came to a head—a dramatic confrontation that would change everything.

It started innocently enough, with a simple disagreement over a project deadline. But as tempers flared and emotions ran high, the situation quickly spiraled out of control. Harsh words were exchanged, accusations hurled like weapons in a battle of wills.

Ella stood her ground, her voice shaking with emotion as she defended herself against Lena's relentless onslaught. But no matter how hard she fought, it seemed that Lena was determined to tear her down, to strip away every last shred of her confidence and self-worth.

And as the confrontation reached its climax, Alex found himself faced with an impossible choice—should he intervene and risk alienating Lena, or should he stand by and watch as Ella suffered?

But as the confrontation reached its crescendo, a sense of clarity washed over him like a wave crashing against the shore. He realized that he couldn't stand idly by and watch as Ella was torn apart by Lena's cruelty. He had to take a stand, to defend the woman he loved with every fiber of his being.

With a resolve born of desperation and determination, Alex stepped forward, his voice ringing out clear and strong above the chaos. "That's enough, Lena," he declared, his eyes flashing with a fierce determination. "You've gone too far this time. Ella deserves better than this, and so do you."

Lena's eyes widened in shock at Alex's intervention, her façade of confidence momentarily shattered by his unexpected defiance. For a moment, it seemed as if she might lash out in anger, but then, to everyone's surprise, she simply turned on her heel and stormed out of the room, leaving behind a trail of stunned silence in her wake.

And in that moment, as the tension slowly began to dissipate and the storm clouds of conflict parted, Alex knew that he had made the right choice. He had chosen love over fear, courage over complacency, and in doing so, he had changed the course of their destinies forever.

As he turned to face Ella, a tentative smile tugging at the corners of his lips, he saw the flicker of gratitude and relief in her eyes. And in that shared moment of understanding, they knew that whatever challenges lay ahead, they would face them together, united in their love and determination to overcome whatever obstacles stood in their way.

"A Crossroads: Confronting Consequences and Embracing Growth"

CHAPTER SEVEN

Choices and Consequences

A Crossroads

Ella's heart raced as she stared at the email notification on her screen, her hands trembling with uncertainty. It was a message from Lena, requesting a private meeting to discuss the events of the previous day's confrontation. And Ella knew that whatever lay ahead, it would be anything but easy.

As she sat in the dimly lit conference room, waiting for Lena to arrive, a sense of foreboding settled over her like a heavy shroud. She knew that this meeting could very well determine the course of her future at Tech Innovations, and the thought filled her with a potent mix of fear and determination.

When Lena finally entered the room, her expression was inscrutable, her eyes betraying nothing of her true intentions. "Ella," she said, her voice cool and composed. "I trust you received my email?"

Ella nodded, her throat dry with apprehension. "Yes, Lena, I did," she replied, trying to keep her voice steady despite the tumult of emotions swirling inside her. "I'm here to listen."

Lena regarded her for a moment, her gaze piercing and intense. "Good," she said, her tone unreadable. "Because what I have to say is of the utmost importance, both for you and for the future of this company."

Ella braced herself for whatever was to come, steeling her nerves against the onslaught of Lena's words. But nothing could have prepared her for what came next.

"I want you off the project, Ella," Lena said, her voice cold and authoritative. "Effective immediately."

Ella felt as if the ground had been ripped out from beneath her feet, leaving her adrift in a sea of uncertainty. She had known that Lena was unhappy with her performance, but she had never imagined that it would come to this.

"But why?" she asked, her voice trembling with disbelief. "I've been working so hard, putting in long hours to make this project a success. Why would you want to remove me now?"

Lena's expression softened slightly, a hint of pity flickering in her eyes. "Because I can't trust you, Ella," she said, her voice tinged with regret. "You've shown a blatant disregard for authority, undermining my leadership at every turn. And I simply can't afford to have someone like that on my team."

Ella felt as if she had been punched in the gut, the weight of Lena's words crushing her spirit beneath their weight. She had always prided herself on her dedication and professionalism, and to be accused of such betrayal was a blow she wasn't sure she could recover from.

But amidst the chaos and confusion, a flicker of defiance ignited within her, a determination to fight back against the injustice of Lena's accusations. She knew that she couldn't let herself be pushed around, not when so much was at stake.

"I won't accept this, Lena," Ella declared, her voice ringing out clear and strong in the tense silence of the conference room. "I won't let you push me out without a fight."

Lena's eyes narrowed at Ella's defiance, her expression hardening with resolve. "You have no choice in the matter, Ella," she retorted, her voice dripping with disdain. "I hold all the cards here, and I won't hesitate to use them if you force my hand."

But Ella refused to back down, her resolve unshakeable in the face of Lena's threats. "You may have the power to remove me from the project," she conceded, her voice unwavering, "but you can't erase the work I've done or the contributions I've made. And if you think I'll go quietly into the night, you're sorely mistaken."

There was a moment of tense silence as the gravity of Ella's words hung in the air like a dare, challenging Lena to make her next move. And then, to everyone's surprise, Lena's mask of composure slipped, revealing a flicker of uncertainty beneath the surface.

"You're making a mistake, Ella," Lena said, her voice surprisingly soft. "You have no idea what you're up against."

But Ella remained undeterred, her determination burning bright like a beacon in the darkness. "Maybe not," she conceded, her voice steady with resolve, "but I won't let fear dictate my actions. I'll face whatever consequences come my way, knowing that I stood up for what's right."

With that, Ella rose from her seat, her head held high despite the weight of uncertainty pressing down on her shoulders. She knew that the road ahead would be difficult, fraught with obstacles and challenges at every turn. But she also knew that she couldn't let fear hold her back, not when so much was at stake.

As she left the conference room behind her, a sense of empowerment washed over her like a wave crashing against the shore. She may not have all the answers, but she knew that she had made the right choice, and that was enough to carry her forward into the unknown.

And as she stepped out into the bustling chaos of the office, the sound of ringing phones and clacking keyboards filling the air around her, she felt a renewed sense of purpose coursing through her veins. Whatever lay ahead, she would face it with courage and determination, knowing that no matter what challenges awaited her, she would overcome them with grace and dignity.

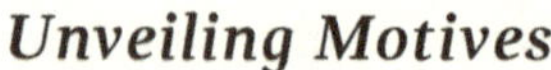

Unveiling Motives

As the days passed, the tension in the office seemed to reach a boiling point, the atmosphere thick with anticipation and uncertainty. And amidst the chaos, Lena's true motives began to surface, shedding light on her actions throughout the story and forcing Ella to confront her own insecurities.

It started innocently enough, with a chance encounter in the break room. Ella was lost in thought, her mind still reeling from her confrontation with Lena, when she overheard snippets of conversation between two colleagues.

"Did you hear about Lena's latest power play?" one whispered, her voice tinged with disbelief. "It seems she's been gunning for Ella's position all along."

Ella's heart skipped a beat at the mention of Lena's name, her mind racing with a whirlwind of emotions. Could it be true? Had Lena been plotting against her from the very beginning?

Determined to get to the bottom of things, Ella set out to uncover the truth, her instincts guiding her towards a confrontation that would change everything.

But as she delved deeper into Lena's past, what she uncovered shocked her to the core. It seemed that Lena's motives were far more sinister than she had ever imagined, driven not by a desire for power or prestige, but by a deep-seated sense of insecurity and inadequacy.

Lena had always been the golden child, the one destined for greatness from the moment she set foot in the company. But beneath her polished exterior lay a well of self-doubt and fear, a fear of failure and rejection that drove her to extreme measures to protect her fragile ego.

And as Ella pieced together the puzzle of Lena's past, she couldn't help but feel a twinge of sympathy for the woman who had made her life a living hell. For in Lena, she saw a reflection of her own insecurities, a reminder of the vulnerability that lurked within us all.

But amidst the revelations and the turmoil, a sense of clarity began to emerge—a realization that the only way to break free from the cycle of fear and insecurity was to confront it head-on, to embrace the uncertainty of the unknown and forge a new path forward.

Armed with this newfound insight, Ella set out to confront Lena once and for all, knowing that whatever lay ahead, she would face it with courage and determination, secure in the knowledge that she was stronger than she had ever realized.

And as she stood before Lena, her heart pounding with anticipation, she knew that this was a confrontation that would change everything—a confrontation that would force them both to confront the demons that haunted them and emerge stronger on the other side.

Confronting Consequences

As the dust settled and the echoes of their confrontation faded into the ether, Ella found herself grappling with the weight of the choices she had made. The air in the office was heavy with tension, the aftermath of their showdown leaving a palpable sense of unease lingering in its wake.

Alone in her cubicle, Ella sat in silence, her mind awash with a whirlwind of emotions. She couldn't shake the feeling that she had opened a Pandora's box, unleashing forces beyond her control that threatened to consume her whole.

But amidst the chaos and confusion, a sense of clarity began to emerge—a realization that the only way forward was to confront the consequences of her choices head-on, to embrace the uncertainty of the unknown and forge a new path forward.

With a deep breath and a steely resolve, Ella rose from her seat, determined to face whatever lay ahead with courage and dignity. She knew that the road ahead would be fraught with obstacles and challenges, but she also knew that she had the strength and resilience to overcome them.

As she made her way through the maze of cubicles, the weight of responsibility pressing down on her shoulders, Ella couldn't help but feel a sense of liberation wash over her. For the first time in her life, she was truly free—free to chart her own course, free to pursue her own dreams, free to be herself without fear or reservation.

And as she stepped out into the bustling chaos of the office, the sound of ringing phones and clacking keyboards filling the air around her, Ella felt a renewed sense of purpose coursing through her veins. Whatever lay ahead, she would face it with courage and determination, knowing that no matter what challenges awaited her, she would overcome them with grace and dignity.

As Ella grapples with the aftermath of her confrontation with Lena, several incidents unfold, further shaping her journey of self-discovery and personal growth:

Office Gossip:

Rumors and whispers spread like wildfire through the office following Ella and Lena's confrontation, with colleagues speculating about what transpired between them. Ella finds herself the subject of scrutiny and judgment, adding to the pressure she already feels.

Support from Colleagues:

Despite the tension in the office, Ella finds unexpected allies among her colleagues who offer words of encouragement and solidarity. Their support bolsters her spirits and reminds her that she's not alone in her struggles.

Professional Repercussions:

As word of the confrontation reaches upper management, Ella faces the prospect of disciplinary action or even termination. The uncertainty of her future at Tech Innovations looms large, adding to her anxiety and uncertainty.

Reflection and Soul-Searching:

Alone in her apartment, Ella takes time to reflect on the events that have transpired and the choices she's made. She delves deep into her own thoughts and emotions, confronting her fears and insecurities head-on.

Heart-to-Heart with Alex:

Seeking solace and guidance, Ella reaches out to Alex for support. In a heart-to-heart conversation, they discuss the events of the past few days and their implications for their relationship. Alex reassures Ella of his unwavering support, strengthening their bond in the face of adversity.

Epiphany and Resolution:

Through introspection and soul-searching, Ella experiences a moment of clarity—a realization that she is stronger and more resilient than she ever thought possible. With newfound resolve, she commits to facing whatever challenges lie ahead with courage and determination.

These incidents not only serve to advance the plot but also deepen Ella's character development, showcasing her resilience and inner strength as she navigates the aftermath of her choices. They contribute to the emotional depth of the narrative, setting the stage for Ella's continued growth and transformation.

And in that moment of self-discovery and personal growth, Ella knew that she was ready to embrace whatever the future held, secure in the knowledge that she had the strength and resilience to face whatever came her way.

"A Journey Within: Rediscovering Strength in Unity"

CHAPTER EIGHT

REDEMPTION AND RESOLUTION

A Journey Within

The echoes of recent conflicts reverberated through Ella's mind, a cacophony of doubt and uncertainty that threatened to drown out her resolve. But amidst the chaos, a flicker of determination ignited within her—a silent promise to herself that she would emerge from the darkness stronger than before.

Alone in her apartment, Ella made a decision—a decision to embark on a journey of self-discovery and redemption, to confront the demons that lurked within the recesses of her soul. With a sense of purpose burning bright within her, she packed a bag and set off for a secluded cabin in the woods—a sanctuary where she could seek solace amidst the tranquility of nature.

As the miles stretched on, Ella found herself lost in thought, the rhythm of the road lulling her into a state of introspection. Memories flashed before her eyes like scenes from a movie—moments of joy and sorrow, triumph and defeat, all woven together into the tapestry of her life.

Arriving at the cabin, Ella was greeted by the crisp scent of pine and the gentle rustle of leaves in the breeze. It was a world apart from the chaos of the city—a haven of peace and serenity where she could finally confront the turmoil that had been raging within her for so long.

Alone in the quiet of the forest, Ella allowed herself to unravel—to peel back the layers of protection she had built around herself and expose the raw vulnerability that lay beneath. She wept for the wounds of the past, for the scars that had yet to heal, and for the fear that had held her captive for far too long.

But amidst the tears and the turmoil, Ella felt a sense of liberation—a weight lifting off her shoulders with each breath she took. For the first time in her life, she allowed herself to be truly vulnerable—to embrace her imperfections and flaws as a testament to her humanity.

As the sun dipped below the horizon and the stars emerged in the night sky, Ella sat by the fire, her heart heavy with the weight of her revelations. But amidst the darkness, a spark of hope flickered within her—a glimmer of light illuminating the path forward.

With the dawn of a new day, Ella emerged from her retreat with a renewed sense of purpose and determination. She knew that the road ahead would be fraught with challenges and obstacles, but she also knew that she had the strength and resilience to face them head-on.

And as she made her way back to the city, the echoes of the forest fading into the distance behind her, Ella felt a sense of clarity wash over her—a sense of redemption and resolution that would guide her on her journey forward.

With each passing mile, Ella felt the weight of the city's chaos lift from her shoulders, replaced by a newfound sense of clarity and purpose. The journey back was not just a physical return but a symbolic transition—a crossing from the wilderness of her introspection to the bustling landscape of her reality.

As she stepped back into the familiar hustle and bustle of the city streets, Ella couldn't help but feel a surge of anticipation coursing through her veins. It was as if the air itself crackled with possibility, promising new beginnings and untold adventures.

Returning to her apartment, Ella found herself surrounded by the remnants of her past—a lifetime's worth of memories and mementos that spoke of the person she used to be. But amidst the clutter and chaos, there was a sense of clarity—a knowing that she was no longer defined by the shadows of her past, but by the light of her own resilience.

With renewed purpose, Ella set about reclaiming her space, clearing away the physical clutter to make room for the emotional clarity that had taken root within her. It was a cathartic process—a shedding of old skin to make way for the new, a symbolic rebirth that mirrored the transformation taking place within her soul.

And as the final remnants of the past were swept away, Ella felt a sense of liberation wash over her—a freedom she had never known before. It was a freedom born not of escape, but of acceptance—a knowing that she was no longer bound by the chains of her past, but free to forge her own path forward.

With each passing day, Ella felt herself growing stronger—more resilient, more confident, more alive. She threw herself into her work with renewed vigor, pouring her heart and soul into every line of code, every pixel of design, every moment of creation.

And amidst the chaos of the office, amidst the clacking of keyboards and the ringing of phones, Ella found herself at peace—a sense of calm amidst the storm, a knowing that she was exactly where she was meant to be.

For in the journey of self-discovery and redemption, Ella had found not just herself, but a sense of purpose and belonging that had eluded her for so long. And as she stood on the threshold of a new beginning, she knew that the best was yet to come.

A Decisive Choice

As Ella embarked on her journey of self-discovery and redemption, she wasn't the only one grappling with the weight of their shared experiences. Across town, in his own corner of the world, Alex found himself confronting his own feelings and making a decisive choice about his future—a choice that would ultimately lead to a resolution of the love triangle and closure for all involved.

For weeks, Alex had been wrestling with his emotions—caught between his loyalty to the company and his growing feelings for Ella. Each day brought new challenges and uncertainties, testing the boundaries of his professionalism and his heart.

But amidst the chaos of his internal struggle, a moment of clarity emerged—a realization that he could no longer ignore the truth of his own desires. And with that realization came a decision—a decision to confront his feelings head-on and make a choice about what he truly wanted.

Taking a deep breath, Alex squared his shoulders and made his way to Ella's desk, his heart pounding in his chest with a mixture of anticipation and fear. He knew that the conversation ahead would not be easy, but he also knew that it was necessary—for both of their sakes.

As he approached, Ella looked up from her work, her eyes widening in surprise at the sight of him standing before her. There was a moment of hesitation, a silent acknowledgment of the weight of the words that hung between them, before Alex spoke, his voice steady with conviction.

"Ella, we need to talk," he began, his words hanging in the air like a tangible force. "About us, about everything that's been happening between us."

And as he spoke, Alex laid bare his heart, baring his soul to Ella in a way he had never done before. He spoke of his feelings for her, of the way she had captured his heart and changed his world in ways he could never have imagined.

But amidst the confession, there was also a sense of responsibility—a recognition of the complexities of their situation and the implications of their choices. And as Alex spoke, he made it clear that he understood the consequences of his actions, that he was prepared to face whatever challenges lay ahead.

And as Ella listened, her own heart aching with the weight of their shared truths, she knew that this was a moment of reckoning—a moment that would define the course of their future together. And as she met Alex's gaze, her eyes shimmering with unshed tears, she knew that whatever happened next, they would face it together—as partners, as equals, as two souls bound by the unbreakable ties of love.

As Alex's heartfelt confession hung in the air, Ella found herself enveloped in a whirlwind of emotions. She had long suspected the depth of Alex's feelings for her, but hearing them spoken aloud sent a shiver down her spine and ignited a spark of hope in her heart.

But amidst the rush of emotions, Ella couldn't ignore the weight of their reality—the tangled web of professional boundaries and personal desires that threatened to ensnare them both. She knew that Alex's declaration was not just a proclamation of love, but a call to action—a challenge to navigate the treacherous waters of their shared feelings with courage and integrity.

Taking a moment to gather her thoughts, Ella met Alex's gaze with a mixture of vulnerability and determination. "Alex," she began, her voice trembling slightly with emotion, "I... I don't know what to say."

But before she could continue, Alex reached out and took her hand in his, his touch sending a jolt of electricity coursing through her veins. "You don't have to say anything, Ella," he said softly, his eyes searching hers for any sign of understanding. "I just needed you to know... how I feel."

And in that moment, as they stood there, hand in hand, the weight of their shared truth hanging heavy in the air, Ella felt a sense of clarity wash over her—a knowing that whatever challenges lay ahead, they would face them together, united in their love and their commitment to one another.

With a silent nod of understanding, Ella squeezed Alex's hand tightly, her heart overflowing with gratitude and affection. And as they stood there, lost in the moment, the world around them faded into insignificance, leaving only the two of them and the promise of a future filled with endless possibilities.

Strength in Unity

As they stood together, the weight of their past struggles began to lift, replaced by a newfound sense of camaraderie and understanding. Each of them had faced their own demons and emerged stronger for it, and now, united in their shared experiences, they were ready to face whatever the future held.

For Ella, the journey had been one of self-discovery and empowerment. She had faced her fears head-on, confronting the insecurities that had held her back for so long. And now, standing tall and unafraid, she was ready to embrace the opportunities that lay before her, confident in her abilities and her worth.

Alex, too, had undergone a transformation of his own. He had grappled with his feelings for Ella, torn between his professional responsibilities and his desire for something more. But now, having made his choice and laid his heart on the line, he felt a sense of peace wash over him—a peace born of honesty and authenticity.

And Lena, with her past mistakes behind her, looked towards the future with renewed hope and determination. She had learned the value of humility and compassion, and now, armed with these newfound virtues, she was ready to rebuild what she had lost and forge a new path forward.

As they shared a moment of quiet reflection, the air around them seemed to hum with possibility. The future was uncertain, but they faced it with open hearts and minds, knowing that whatever challenges lay ahead, they would face them together.

And as they turned towards the horizon, a sense of optimism filled their hearts—a belief in the power of love to conquer even the greatest of obstacles. For in the end, it was their bonds of friendship and camaraderie that had seen them through, and it was these same bonds that would carry them forward into the bright unknown.

"Fulfillment Found: Ella and Alex's Journey to Contentment"

CHAPTER NINE

The Code of Love

A Fulfilling Conclusion

As the final chapter of their journey unfolded, Ella found herself standing at the precipice of a new beginning, her heart filled with a sense of fulfillment and contentment. The trials and tribulations she had faced had led her to this moment, and now, as she looked back on the path she had traveled, she knew that every step had been worth it.

In her career, Ella had found success beyond her wildest dreams. The once timid junior developer had blossomed into a confident and accomplished professional, her skills honed by years of hard work and dedication. With each new challenge she faced, she rose to the occasion, proving herself time and time again in the competitive world of tech.

But it wasn't just her career that had flourished—it was her relationship with Alex as well. What had begun as a tentative friendship had blossomed into something deeper and more profound, a love that transcended the boundaries of time and space. Together, they had weathered the storms of life, their bond growing stronger with each passing day.

And now, as she stood on the threshold of a new chapter in her life, Ella knew that she had finally found her place in the world. She was no longer defined by her past insecurities or her fears of inadequacy. Instead, she was defined by her resilience, her determination, and her unwavering belief in herself.

With Alex by her side, Ella felt invincible—as if together, they could conquer anything that came their way. Their love was a source of strength and inspiration, a guiding light that illuminated the darkest corners of their souls and brought warmth to even the coldest of nights.

As the final pages of their story unfolded, Ella found herself filled with gratitude—for the challenges that had tested her, for the friendships that had sustained her, and most of all, for the love that had transformed her life in ways she could never have imagined.

And as she looked towards the future, she did so with a sense of peace and contentment, knowing that no matter what trials lay ahead, she would face them with courage and grace. For she had found her purpose, her passion, and her place in the world—and nothing could ever take that away from her.

With each passing day, Ella and Alex found themselves more deeply entrenched in their shared journey, their love growing stronger with every moment they spent together. It was as if they were two pieces of a puzzle, each fitting perfectly into the other, creating a picture of completeness and harmony that neither could have ever imagined.

As they navigated the complexities of their relationship, they did so with open hearts and open minds, their bond strengthened by the trials they had faced together. Gone were the doubts and insecurities that had plagued them in the past, replaced by a profound sense of trust and understanding that anchored them to each other like ships in a stormy sea.

Together, they faced the future with courage and conviction, knowing that whatever challenges lay ahead, they would overcome them together. Their love was a beacon of hope in a world filled with uncertainty, a guiding light that led them through even the darkest of times.

And as they looked towards the horizon, they did so with a sense of excitement and anticipation, eager to see where the road ahead would take them. For they knew that as long as they had each other, they could weather any storm and conquer any obstacle that stood in their way.

In the end, it was their love that defined them—a love that was as boundless as the sky and as eternal as the stars. And as they embarked on the next chapter of their journey, they did so with a sense of joy and gratitude, knowing that they were truly blessed to have found each other in a world filled with chaos and uncertainty.

In this concluding chapter of the book, Ella's journey reaches its culmination as she finds fulfillment in her career and her relationship with Alex. Through her growth and transformation, readers are reminded of the power of love and perseverance to overcome even the greatest of obstacles. And as Ella looks towards the future with hope and excitement, readers are left with a sense of optimism and possibility, knowing that no matter what challenges they may face, they too can find their own version of happily ever after.

Lessons Learned, Strength Found

In the closing chapters of their story, Ella and Alex found themselves not only basking in the warmth of their love but also reflecting on the lessons they had learned and the growth they had experienced along the way. Their journey had been marked by trials and tribulations, but through it all, they had emerged stronger and more resilient than ever before.

As they looked back on the challenges they had faced, they realized that each obstacle had been an opportunity for growth, each setback a chance to learn and evolve. They had navigated the complexities of workplace politics, confronted their own insecurities, and weathered the storm of external pressures—all while holding onto each other with unwavering determination.

Their relationship had been tested in ways they never could have imagined, but with each challenge, their bond had only grown stronger. They had learned to communicate openly and honestly, to trust in each other's strength and resilience, and to lean on each other for support when the world seemed to be crumbling around them.

And now, as they stood on the threshold of a new chapter in their lives, they did so with a sense of optimism and excitement, knowing that whatever the future held, they were ready to face it together. Their love was a beacon of hope in a world filled with uncertainty, a source of strength and inspiration that would carry them through even the darkest of times.

As they looked towards the horizon, they knew that their journey was far from over. There would be challenges ahead, obstacles to overcome, and moments of doubt and fear. But they also knew that as long as they had each other, they could weather any storm and conquer any obstacle that stood in their way.

For in the end, it wasn't the challenges they faced or the trials they endured that defined them—it was the strength of their love, the resilience of their spirit, and the unwavering commitment they had to each other. And as they embarked on the next chapter of their journey, they did so with hearts full of hope and a sense of purpose that could only come from knowing that they had found their forever in each other's arms.

A Hopeful Conclusion

As the final pages of their journey unfolded, Ella and Alex found themselves surrounded by a sense of peace and contentment. Their story had reached its conclusion, but the lessons they had learned and the love they had shared would live on forever in the hearts of those who had followed their journey.

For Ella and Alex, the end of one chapter marked the beginning of another—a chapter filled with endless possibilities and boundless opportunities. They knew that there would be challenges ahead, obstacles to overcome, and moments of doubt and fear. But they also knew that as long as they had each other, they could face whatever the future held with courage and grace.

And so, as they looked towards the horizon, they did so with hearts full of hope and optimism, knowing that their love would be the guiding light that would lead them through even the darkest of times. For they had learned that love was not just a fleeting emotion, but a force of nature—a force that could move mountains and conquer all obstacles in its path.

As the final words of their story faded into the distance, readers were left with a sense of optimism and the belief that love truly does conquer all. For in the end, it wasn't the challenges they faced or the trials they endured that mattered—it was the love they shared, a love that would endure for all eternity.

And so, as readers closed the book on Ella and Alex's journey, they did so with a sense of peace and fulfillment, knowing that love had triumphed in the end. And as they looked towards their own futures, they did so with hearts full of hope and the belief that no matter what challenges lay ahead, love would always be there to light the way.

In this final part of the book, readers are left with a sense of optimism and the belief that love truly does conquer all. As Ella and Alex's journey comes to a close, they are reminded that love is the most powerful force in the universe—a force that can overcome any obstacle and triumph over even the greatest of challenges. And as readers close the book on their story, they do so with a sense of hope and the knowledge that no matter what trials they may face, love will always be there to guide them through.

"In the tapestry of life, love is the thread that binds us together, weaving our stories into a masterpiece of hope and resilience."

- Ayush Gemini

Epilogue

As the sun sets over the horizon, casting a golden glow over the bustling streets of Silicon Valley, our protagonists—Ella, Alex, and Lena—find themselves at a crossroads, their journey of love and ambition reaching its bittersweet conclusion. In the wake of heartache and triumph, they stand on the precipice of a new beginning, their hearts heavy with the weight of the choices they've made and the paths they've chosen to follow.

For Ella, the journey has been one of self-discovery and personal growth, a rollercoaster ride of highs and lows that have shaped her into the woman she is today. From the depths of self-doubt to the heights of professional success, she has weathered the storm with grace and resilience, emerging stronger and more confident than ever before.

As she looks back on the twists and turns of her journey, Ella finds solace in the knowledge that every obstacle she faced was a stepping stone to a brighter future. With Alex by her side, she feels invincible, ready to take on whatever challenges lie ahead with courage and determination.

Meanwhile, Alex grapples with the weight of his own choices, torn between his loyalty to Ella and his sense of duty to his career. For years, he has sacrificed his own happiness in pursuit of success, burying his true feelings beneath a facade of professionalism and ambition.

But as he looks into Ella's eyes, he realizes that he can no longer deny the depth of his love for her. With a sense of clarity and purpose, he vows to stand by her side, come what may, ready to face the future together with unwavering commitment and devotion.

And then there's Lena, the enigmatic project manager whose ambitions threatened to tear their world apart. As she reflects on the events that led to this moment, she finds herself grappling with a sense of regret and longing, wondering if she could have chosen a different path—one filled with love and happiness rather than ambition and power.

In the aftermath of their tumultuous journey, Ella, Alex, and Lena find themselves drawn together by a shared sense of understanding and forgiveness. Despite the scars of the past, they recognize that their bond runs deeper than the trials they've faced, transcending the boundaries of love and ambition to forge a connection that will endure for a lifetime.

As they gather together one last time, beneath the glow of the city lights, they raise a toast to new beginnings and fresh starts, ready to embark on the next chapter of their lives with hope and optimism in their hearts.

For in the end, they realize that love is not just about finding the right person or achieving professional success—it's about embracing the journey, with all its ups and downs, and finding joy in the moments of connection and understanding that make life worth living.

As the night fades into dawn, casting a soft light over the city, Ella, Alex, and Lena bid farewell to the past and look towards the future with renewed hope and determination. With each step they take, they leave behind the shadows of their past selves, ready to embrace the possibilities that lie ahead.

For Ella, the future holds endless promise—a world of opportunity and adventure waiting to be explored. With Alex by her side, she feels ready to take on whatever challenges come their way, secure in the knowledge that their love will see them through even the darkest of times.

And as they walk hand in hand into the sunrise, they know that their journey is far from over. There will be obstacles to overcome, trials to face, and moments of doubt and fear. But together, they are unstoppable, bound by a love that transcends all boundaries and a bond that will endure for eternity.

Meanwhile, Lena finds herself standing at a crossroads, grappling with the choices that led her to this moment. As she looks out over the city skyline, she feels a sense of peace wash over her, knowing that she has finally found the courage to let go of her ambitions and embrace the true desires of her heart.

With a renewed sense of purpose, Lena vows to chart a new course for herself, one filled with love, happiness, and fulfillment. And as she takes the first steps towards a brighter future, she knows that she will always carry the lessons of her past with her, guiding her along the path to self-discovery and personal growth.

And so, as the sun rises over Silicon Valley, illuminating the city with its golden light, our protagonists—Ella, Alex, and Lena—embrace the dawn of a new day with open hearts and minds. For they know that no matter what challenges lie ahead, they will face them together, bound by a love that knows no bounds and a friendship that will last a lifetime.

As they set out on their respective journeys, they carry with them the memories of their past adventures—the triumphs and tribulations, the laughter and tears—that have shaped them into the people they are today. And as they look towards the horizon, they do so with a sense of hope and optimism, knowing that the best is yet to come.

For in the end, they realize that it is not the destination that matters, but the journey itself—the lessons learned, the friendships forged, and the love that binds us all together. And as they step into the unknown, they do so with hearts full of gratitude and a sense of wonder, ready to embrace whatever the future may hold.

"Like lines of code in the grand program of life, our journey intertwines with others, creating a tapestry of love, ambition, and discovery. And as we navigate the complexities of our shared humanity, may we always remember that in the end, it is the connections we forge and the hearts we touch that truly define our legacy"

- Ayush Gemini

About The Author

Ayush Gemini, also known by the pseudonym Ayush Rastogi, is a software engineer by profession and a passionate writer by heart. With a penchant for self-help, motivational literature, and love stories, Ayush finds inspiration in the intricate complexities of the human experience.

Having embarked on his writing journey, Ayush released his debut book, "The Wealthy Habits: How to Build a Rich Life," last year, offering insights into personal finance and the pursuit of a fulfilling lifestyle. Now, with "Cracking the Code of Heart: A Silicon Valley Love Triangle," Ayush delves into the realm of fiction, exploring themes of love, ambition, and self-discovery against the backdrop of Silicon Valley.

When he's not immersed in code or crafting captivating stories, Ayush can be found indulging in his love for literature, exploring new ideas, and seeking inspiration from the world around him. He resides in India with his family, where he continues to pursue his passions and share his unique perspective with the world.

Author's Note

Dear Reader,

As I reflect on the journey of writing "Cracking the Code of Heart: A Silicon Valley Love Triangle," I am filled with a sense of gratitude and humility. This story has been a labor of love—a culmination of countless hours of writing, rewriting, and deep introspection.

At its core, this book is a tribute to the human experience—the triumphs, the trials, and the tangled web of emotions that make us who we are. Through the lives of Ella, Alex, and Lena, I sought to explore the complexities of love, ambition, and personal growth in the unique context of Silicon Valley.

While the characters and events in this story are fictional, the themes they grapple with are deeply rooted in the realities of our world. From the challenges of navigating workplace dynamics to the complexities of romantic relationships, each element of this tale is inspired by the experiences of real people in real situations.

As you journey through the pages of this book, I encourage you to reflect on your own experiences and insights. May you find moments of resonance and connection, and may the story of Ella, Alex, and Lena inspire you to embrace the complexities of life with courage and grace.

Thank you for joining me on this adventure. Your support and readership mean the world to me, and I am grateful for the opportunity to share this story with you.

With warmest regards,
Ayush Gemini (Ayush Rastogi)

Share Your Feedback

Your feedback is invaluable to me as an author, and I would love to hear your thoughts, reviews, or feedback on "Cracking the Code of Heart: A Silicon Valley Love Triangle." Whether you enjoyed the book, have suggestions for improvement, or simply want to share your favorite moments, your input is greatly appreciated.

Please feel free to reach out to me directly via email at ayushgemini13@gmail.com.

I look forward to hearing from you and engaging in discussions about the book!

Thank you for taking the time to read "Cracking the Code of Heart." Your support means the world to me, and I'm grateful for the opportunity to connect with readers like you.

Warm regards,
Ayush Gemini (Ayush Rastogi)

www.ingramcontent.com/pod-product-compliance
Lightning Source LLC
LaVergne TN
LVHW041126150826
845673LV00007B/2191

* 9 7 9 8 8 9 3 6 3 1 6 3 0 *